2015

This Book
Belongs To:

Tommy.
Mackie

Grammy & Papa

Have a Cool day!   10/1/15
Tim Ostermey

Snowball's
Antarctic
Adventures

by Master Photographer
Tim Ostermeyer

Way down in Antarctica, south as can be,
Some emperor penguins have set off to sea.
Snowball and his family all hope to find
Adventure and friends of the very best kind.

Dad joins the family after his swim.
Both Mom and Snowball are glad to see him.
"Have you decided which way we should go?"
"That's the direction - I checked, so I know."

They all reach solid ice with their sweet little son.
All ready for friends who can come join the fun.
But first Snowball needs some more time to grow,
Before he can go out and play in the snow.

Snowball likes to sit on his mom's or dad's feet,
While the other goes out to find something to eat.
He stays warm and eats here - there's just enough space.
Why venture out from his favorite place?

No matter which way he looks, or how far he can see,
There is snow and some water, but not one single tree.
"Look at the penguins jump out of the sea!
I hope that a few of them come visit me."

"Snowball, someone's coming that you'll want to meet!
Be brave now, and venture out - off my feet."

But the visit is no fun for Snowball at all.
The friend is rough and unkind, and Snowball is small.
His parents stand up for him, they don't pretend
That there is no problem - it is their son they defend.

"We'll start an adventure together today;
So don't turn back, Snowball, or go the wrong way.

First they see penguins who form one long line.
The march of the penguins - so wonderfully fine!
"Wow!" Snowball thinks, "they're all family of mine."

"So far everyone's like you, but there's so much more,"
Mom and Dad told him, "We will help you explore.
We'll travel together, so you don't get lost.
You won't want to miss this trip at any cost."

But there is so far to walk, and so much to see,
Snowball whispers, "I am tired Mom, please carry me."
Mom replies, "You are rather heavy, I should charge you a fee."
"Just for a while, mom, I am real light. You will see."

As he tires of walking, Snowball wishes to fly.
"You can't soar through the air," says Dad.
"I'll tell you why.
Because penguins have wings made to swim,
And not to fly."
Snowball was sad, and he wanted to cry.

Did you know
that Emperor
Penguins ...

Do not have nests

Do not live on land

Egg hatches on
Mother or Father's feet

Place themselves
on thick ice
so the chicks
will not fall into sea

March up to 70 miles
to the unfrozen sea
for food

Eat fish, krill, shrimp
and squid

Adults are 4 feet tall
and weigh 80 lb

Baby chicks do
not have waterproof
feathers

There are two ways to travel down here.
Use your stomach as a sled, and you'll go far and near.
And you can still walk - it's not really so rare,
Try not to slip on the ice, or hurt your eyes with its bad glare.

They see a tall penguin stop to sing one cold night.
But his voice is quite harsh and it doesn't sound right.
Some penguins just leave him before he is done.
Without any earplugs, it isn't much fun.

Snowball's friends join the trip now and they like to run.
Exploring the continent of Antarctica is lots of fun.
It's warm for Antarctica, and the ice is somewhat brittle.
The breeze from their running helps cool them a little.

"We're growing up fast from our parent's good feeding.
Call him Bowlingball, not Snowball," the friends are all pleading.
"You're all big and round," Mother says with a smile.
"But I will still call him Snowball for quite a while."

They saw a strange penguin as they walked on.
Snowball was glad Mom and Dad were along.
"Why is he different. Does he need a shave?
It's a Chinstrap penguin, just say 'hi' and wave."

Look at this beach - it has snow not sand!
This is what you find on the Antarctic coastland.

How many penguins can you find?
If you say four penguins, you are far behind.
Look in the snow and water, and then combine.
The total number of penguins is two times nine.

"Look! Thousands of chinstraps must live on this beach.
Yes son, but they're high on a cliff, too hard to reach."

"Right now we will see him while staying low,
Someday you'll be bigger to greet him,
And then we will let you go."

Did you know
that Chinstrap
Penguins ...

Get their name from
the black band on
their chin

Are 2 feet tall

Weigh 10 lb

Feed on krill & fish

Live 15-20 Years

Populate Antarctica
with 13 million

Live on large icebergs

Can dive underwater
to 230 feet

Dives are less
than 30 seconds

Snowball and his friends really love to explore.
They continue to run - they can see so much more.
What can they locate and identify?
"Wow! Look at that bird! It can really soar high."

Did you know that
the Kelp Gull ...

Has white head, upper
wing is black, lower wing is
white, Bill is yellow with red
slot

Feathers were used for
fashionable clothing in 1800's

Eats small fish, rodents,
insects, crustaceans,
baby birds

Has long wings that
allows it to spend
several months airborne

Can swallow a puffin or
small wild duck whole

Is the largest gull in the
world

Fly away from their nest
after 50 days

Has a 5 foot
wingspan

"Try to avoid him," says Dad,
"sometimes he'll eat
An egg or small penguin
in his search for meat.
Now he's full of scraps
thrown from the ship's hull -
This very large bird
is called a Kelp gull."

The twenty hour daylight makes young penguins tired.
A nice place to lie down is now so much desired.
But their tiredness so quickly is put out of mind
When they go round a corner and suddenly find....

...A glorious, all natural Antarctic sunset.
Nothing man-made, not a boat or fishnet.

They follow Dad toward blue water serene,
With the loveliest cliffs that they ever have seen.
The Lemaire Channel is rather well known.
Its glaciers and mountains quite often are shown.

Looking out toward the sea,
They see a Minke whale.
He makes quite a splash
Without using his tail.
Snowball and his friends
Enjoy watching him play.
Another fun event of their day.

Did you know that
Minke Whales ...

Have 2 blowholes

Grow to 25 to 30 feet long

Weigh up to 19,000 lb (9.5 tons)

Swim 3-16 miles per hour
(mph), but swim 18-21 mph
when in danger, and
1-6 mph when feeding

Dive up to 20-25 minutes

Live over 20 years

Number 800,000 in the world

Make very loud sounds (152 db,
as loud as a jet taking off)

Have dark skin above
and light skin below

Babies can swim within
30 minutes of birth

As the whale disappears down into the water,
There is no sign of wildlife, not even one otter.
No dolphin, no seabird, no shrimp and no krill,
Only snow-capped mountains, so perfectly still.

So Snowball and his friends continued looking.
It was almost time for dinner and some great cooking.

All of the penguins enjoy the climb.
But, it does take a really long time.
This is because they are hungry.
It is very close to mealtime.

Icebergs have unique shapes and color.
A world without them would be a bit duller.

By now Snowball's tired and a little worn out.
A short rest will help him, there isn't a doubt.

Afterwards, Snowball yells out, "Now I'm ready to go,
For another adventure in the ice and snow.
What wildlife is waiting? I do want to know."

Snowball looked up at the iceberg that is so tall.
Extreme cold weather lets him know it is winter and not fall.
Compared to the iceberg, he is very small.
Snowball knows because of this nice scenery,
That he is in no shopping mall.

Did you know
Icebergs ...

Are pieces of ice that
form on land and float
in the ocean

Vary in size from ice
cube chunks to ice
islands the size of a
small country

Caused the Titanic
ship to sink in 1912

Colors of iceberg are
due to compressed gas
and algae

Can melt and leak
nutrients to plankton,
fish, and sealife that
surround the iceberg

Travel with ocean
currents

"When you swim," Father says,
"Stay alert to the shape of each iceberg,
In case you have need to escape.
This one has a tunnel
That you could swim through,
In case there's a leopard seal
That's chasing you."

The iceberg color is aqua blue,
Without even adding any colored shampoo.
Amazingly, 90% of most icebergs
Are below the water, too.

Antarctica and its icebergs are so very pretty.
It is nothing like you find in the big city.

This is another type of penguin
Called the gentoo.
He has a white mark on his head,
A very interesting hairdo.

Did you know that
Gentoo Penguins ...

Have white stripe on top
of head from eye to eye

Live in large and noisy
breeding colonies

Stand 30 to 35 inches tall

Weigh 13 lbs

Have a very bright
orange beak

Number 300,00 breeding
pairs

Nest on rocky shores making
nests from stones, pebbles,
grass, and sticks

Are agressive and will
fight over stones
or take items from
other nests

The Gentoos are having so much fun swimming together.
Snowball is impressed because
He does not yet have one waterproof feather
To swim underwater, or keep dry in bad weather.

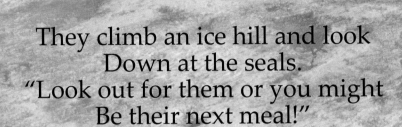

They climb an ice hill and look
Down at the seals.
"Look out for them or you might
Be their next meal!"

Did you know that
Seals...

Have 5 main types:
Leopard, Ross, Crabeater,
Elephant, and Weddell

Live on krill, fish,
and squid

Eat fish
and penguins

Can grow to 16 feet long

Are curious and like
to follow boats to see
what is going on
aboard

Are called bulls when
they're male, cows when
female, and pups when babies

Have been know to attack
and bite humans that
get too close

Shed their skin, or molt,
once a year

What is that big fish far off on the sea?
That is not a fish, can't you even see?
It is an icebreaker ship,
I think that we can all agree.

Did you know
that ...

The Drake Sea near
Antarctica is the roughest
sea in the world

If you traveled on an
icebreaker to get
to Antartica,
you would travel 2 days
in each direction
on this rough sea

The icebreaker has no
rudder to keep the
ship steady

Plus or minus 20 to 30
degrees of side to side
ship rocking can be
expected, which makes
many of the travelers
seasick

Snowball was amazed at the height
Of the waves. It was really quite a sight.
This Cape Petrel bird was also a delight.

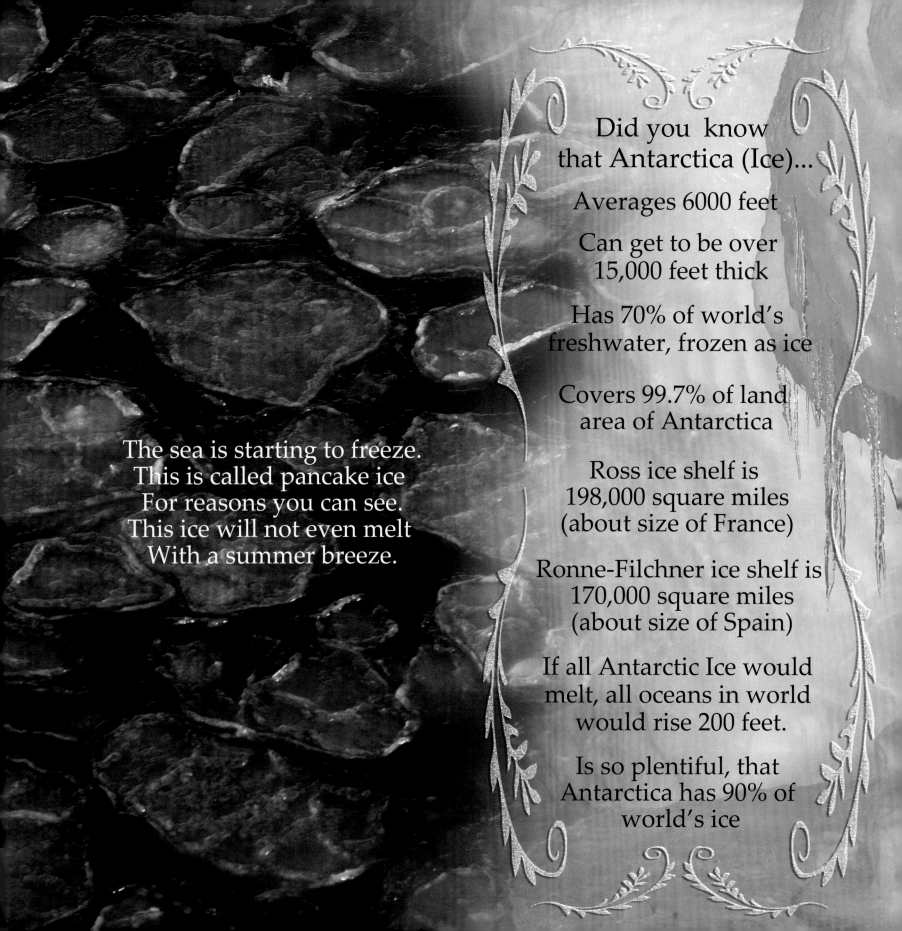

Did you know
that Antarctica (Ice)...

Averages 6000 feet

Can get to be over
15,000 feet thick

Has 70% of world's
freshwater, frozen as ice

Covers 99.7% of land
area of Antarctica

Ross ice shelf is
198,000 square miles
(about size of France)

Ronne-Filchner ice shelf is
170,000 square miles
(about size of Spain)

If all Antarctic Ice would
melt, all oceans in world
would rise 200 feet.

Is so plentiful, that
Antarctica has 90% of
world's ice

The sea is starting to freeze.
This is called pancake ice
For reasons you can see.
This ice will not even melt
With a summer breeze.

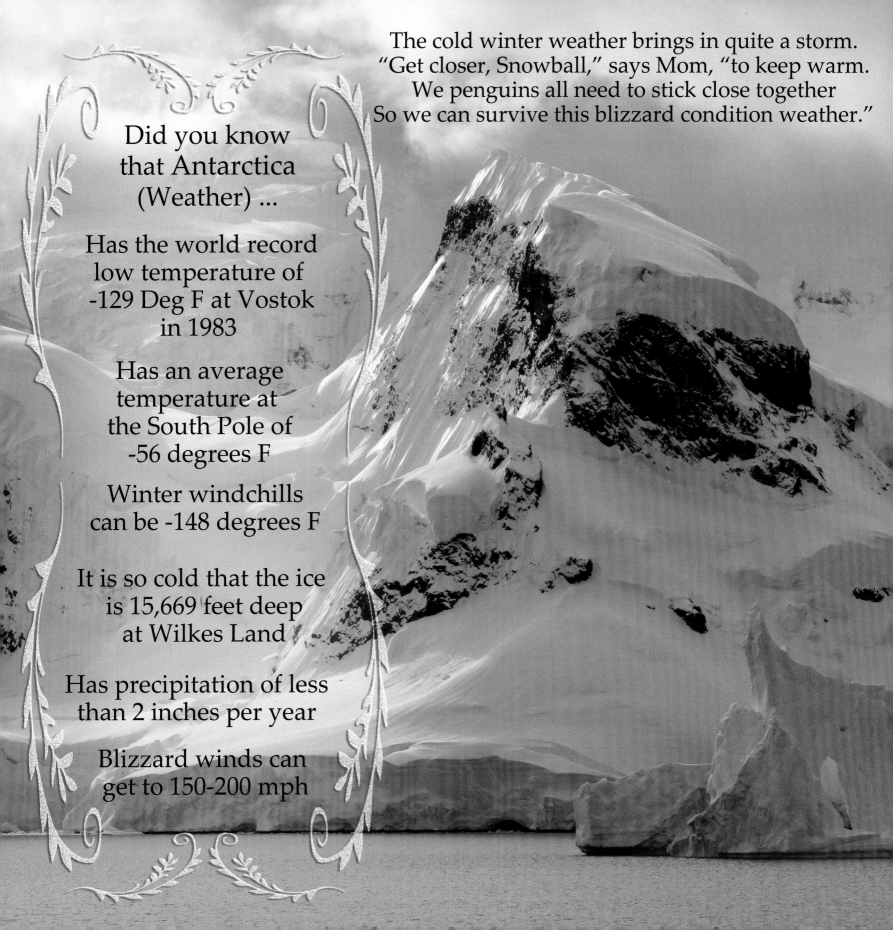

The cold winter weather brings in quite a storm.
"Get closer, Snowball," says Mom, "to keep warm.
We penguins all need to stick close together
So we can survive this blizzard condition weather."

Did you know
that Antarctica
(Weather) ...

Has the world record
low temperature of
-129 Deg F at Vostok
in 1983

Has an average
temperature at
the South Pole of
-56 degrees F

Winter windchills
can be -148 degrees F

It is so cold that the ice
is 15,669 feet deep
at Wilkes Land

Has precipitation of less
than 2 inches per year

Blizzard winds can
get to 150-200 mph

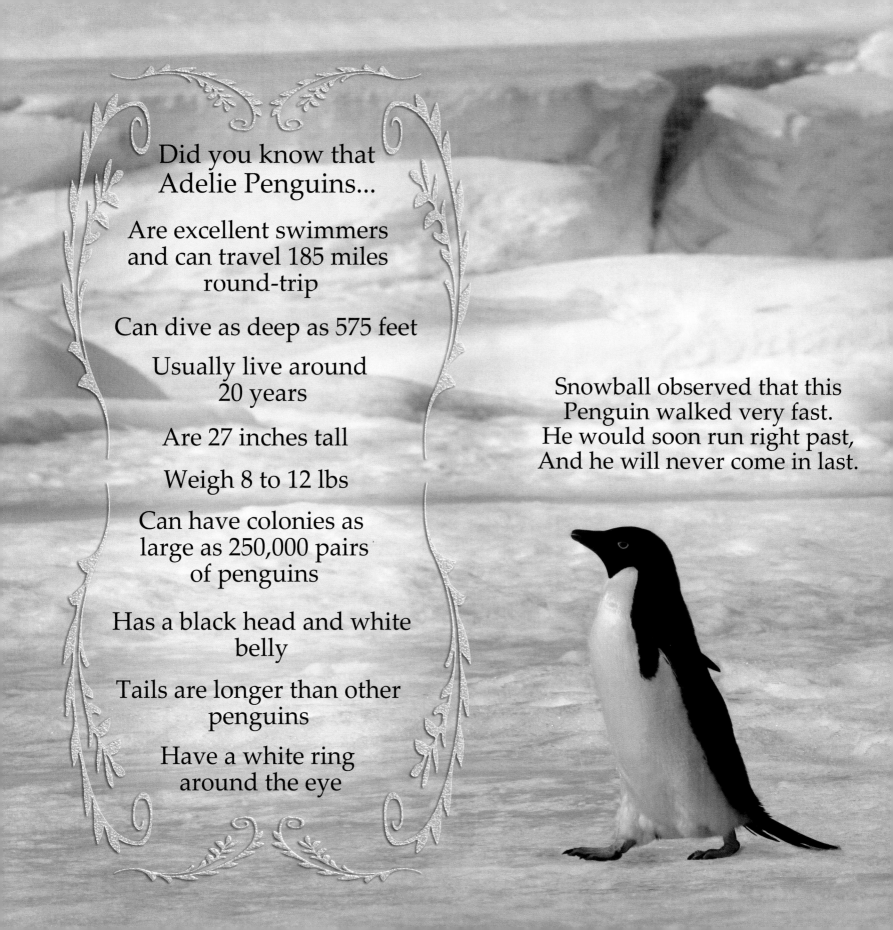

Did you know that
Adelie Penguins...

Are excellent swimmers
and can travel 185 miles
round-trip

Can dive as deep as 575 feet

Usually live around
20 years

Are 27 inches tall

Weigh 8 to 12 lbs

Can have colonies as
large as 250,000 pairs
of penguins

Has a black head and white
belly

Tails are longer than other
penguins

Have a white ring
around the eye

Snowball observed that this
Penguin walked very fast.
He would soon run right past,
And he will never come in last.

Here the Adelie penguins are skiing with no skis.
That looks like fun, as they move quickly and free.
They are happy to be in Antarctica,
where they will not run into a tree.

Snowball peeked around his family.
"These are the strangest creatures of all.
Because of their long legs, long arms,
Big heads, funny looking clothes,
Rubber feet, and
Because they are so tall.
What are they called?"

"These are called humans," said his mother.
"When they come to Antarctica,
They bring cameras and are then
Called tourists.
They really don't have rubber feet,
They are just wearing rubber boots.
Aren't they the coolest."

Did you know that
Antarctic Tourists...

Wear Arctic clothing

Usually have cameras
in front of their faces

Are usually cold

Often spend
$10,000 or more
to travel to Antarctica

Are very lucky people to
see these magnificent
penguins in the wild

Snowball said,
"It was so much fun to find
Various penguins, yes four different kinds.
Whales and seals were not too far behind.
Icebergs, cool ice, and wild weather were
Often combined,
All on the bottom of the earth,
It just blows my mind."

"Snowball was as excited
As a baby penguin could be.
Thanks Mom and Dad for helping me,
Get out of my comfort zone so that we
Could explore Antarctica, in order to see
All the wonderful wildlife and scenery,
That are so awesome in Antarctica.
We saw everything,
But not one single tree."

"Mom and Dad, I love you,
And I also have this.
Get close so I can give you
One really big kiss."

The Author is so Appreciative of the Scenic Beauty & Gorgeous Wildlife That He Has Witnessed in His Travels.

Tim is grateful for his clients; parents, grandparents, teachers, and librarians.

These are the cutest baby animals on earth, Call 1-972-542-7065 to order the whole set.
(Gorgeous baby wildlife photos, Up to 130 facts per book, fun story line, moral messages)

Baby Foxes	Baby Penguins	Baby Tigers	Baby Polar Bears	Baby Snow Monkeys	Baby Ducks	Baby Panda Bears
		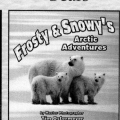			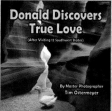	
Sharing	Exploring	Bullying	Going After Dreams	Planning	Finding True Love	Having Fun

Copyright 2011 Tim Ostermeyer - All Rights Reserved

Published by Fun Adventure Wildlife Books

1813 Country Brook Lane
Allen, Texas 75002
1-972-542-7065
www.FunAdventureWildlifeBooks.com
www.ostermeyer-photography.com

Library of Congress Catalog Data on File with Publisher
ISBN: 978-0-9794228-3-6

Printed and Bound in Canada (Friesens of Altona, Manitoba)

Storyline, Photography, Graphic Art, and Cover Design by Tim Ostermeyer
Words by Tim Ostermeyer and Lois Snyder

(Note: Proper grammar for rhyming test is to capitalize the first word of each rhymed line)